Collins

IMPERIAL WAR MUSEUMS

SPIES

MIKE GOULD

So, what do you know about spying?

What comes into your head when you hear the word "spy"?

Following people

Secret agents

Hiding

Guns and gadgets

Danger

War

Disguise

Trust and betrayal

Keeping secrets

Codes and passwords

James Bond

Spying is all around us.

- Have you seen CCTV cameras in the street?

- Who tries to find out if there's going to be a terrorist attack?

- Have you heard of police going **undercover** and pretending to be in a criminal gang to find out information?

Spies sometimes say they work for the **intelligence services**.

When we talk about spying, "intelligence" usually means information or knowledge, rather than being clever. Spies need to know …

- what their enemy is saying and doing

- their enemy's next move

- who is spying on *them*!

Super spies

Spy stories in books, films and on TV are very popular. This fictional secret agent is probably the most famous of all.

Name: Bond, James Bond (also known as "007")

Creator: Ian Fleming

Job: Works for MI6 and his boss M, stopping bad people from taking over the world; has a "licence to kill"

Weapon of choice: Walther PPK Handgun

As seen in: Many books and 23 films, including *Goldfinger* and *Casino Royale*

Inside info

The Bond game *GoldenEye 007* for the Nintendo 64 has sold over eight million copies.

Not all fictional spies are like Bond. Some look more like bank managers or school teachers.

Name: George Smiley

Creator: John le Carré

Job: Senior Intelligence Officer, MI6

Weapon of choice: His memory and his mind

As seen in: TV dramas, films and novels, such as *Tinker Tailor Soldier Spy*

Inside info

Both James Bond and George Smiley were created by writers who actually worked for the British intelligence services.

Of course, there are stories about female spies, too.

Who is this?

Name: Modesty Blaise

Job: Works for British secret service; used to run "The Network" which made her rich but bored

Weapon of choice: Yawara stick or "kongo"; Colt .32 revolver

As seen in: Comic strips in newspapers such as the *Evening Standard*, later in comic books such as *Death Trap* (2007)

And some fictional spies are very young …

Name: Alex Rider

Age: 14

Creator: Anthony Horowitz

Job: Starts to work for British secret service as undercover teenage spy

Weapon of choice: His hands – he's a Black Belt in karate

Seen in: Novels such as *Skeleton Key* and *Eagle Strike*, and the book and film, *Stormbreaker*

In *Stormbreaker*, Alex escapes from two killers on quad bikes armed with flame-throwers!

There are lots more fictional spies and secret agents. Can you think of any others?

A short history of spying

In real life, there have been many spies through the ages.

Queen Elizabeth I's reign (1558–1603)

During the Elizabethan era, England was at war with other countries, including Spain. The Queen also had enemies at home who thought she should not be Queen of England.

She badly needed someone to spy on her enemies.

This man, Sir Francis Walsingham, was her **spymaster**.

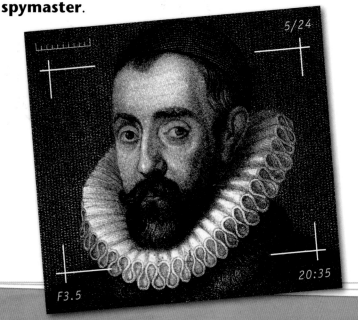

He used his spies to watch the Queen's enemies and to get hold of their secret messages.

He paid some people money for information and used torture to extract it from others.

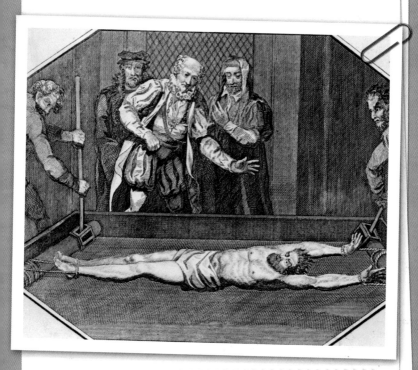

Here is a prisoner on the rack.
The prisoner's body is being pulled and pulled.

First World War (1914–1918) and Second World War (1939–1945)

In both world wars, Britain, France and later Russia (or the Soviet Union as it was later called) and the USA fought Germany and her allies. Spying was an important part of warfare. It was vital to know where the next attack was coming from.

In the Second World War, the British set up a top secret organisation called the **Special Operations Executive (SOE)**. It carried out spying missions in countries occupied by Nazi Germany, such as France.

The Cold War (1945–1991)

After the Second World War, the powerful communist Soviet Union took over much of Eastern Europe. Britain, the USA and other "Western" countries were worried what might happen next. Each side wanted to find out the other's plans. Their spies were very busy.

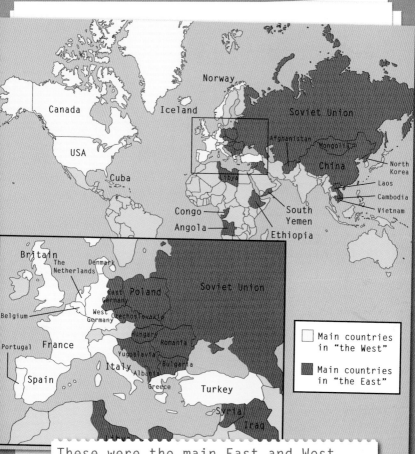

These were the main East and West countries in the Cold War.

Today

Nowadays, many of the enemies have changed, but countries still have spies.

Who do spies work for?

In the UK, if you want to be a spy, you usually work for MI5 or MI6.

MI5 is the **Security Service**. It looks for threats *inside* the UK, such as terrorist plots.

MI6 is also known as the **Secret Intelligence Service (SIS)**. Its job is to work *outside* the UK to find out about external threats to the country.

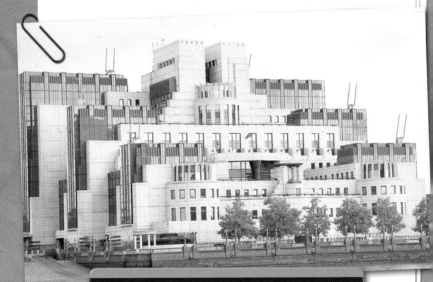

Inside info

This is the MI6 building in London. It is sometimes called "Legoland"!

Other spy organisations

You probably know about the American CIA and FBI from films and television. The CIA works abroad (like MI6) and the FBI works inside the United States.

Do you know the names of any spy organisations in other countries? Where would you find the FSB?

Can you come up with your own name for a spy organisation? What would your logo say?

What do spies do?

There are lots of different spying jobs.

Some of them are based in an office. For example, you might read or listen to secret information in different languages, and translate it.

Other workers are on the ground in this country or overseas. They collect information by living secret lives undercover.

Or you might have a job helping the spies. For example, you might set up computers, cameras or other gadgets. Or you might run a **safe house**, where suspects or witnesses are kept in secret.

Spy skills

So, you want to be a spy … but have you got the right skills for the job?

Can you keep a secret?

To be a British spy you will have to sign the **Official Secrets Act**.

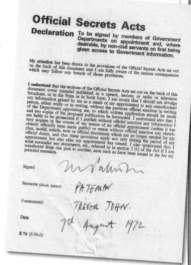

Once you have signed it, there are certain things you *cannot* tell others about.

Some spies are not allowed to tell their families *anything* about their job. They may have to pretend to do a different job altogether.

Can you think of a friend you could rely on to keep a secret *forever*? If so, they might make a good spy!

Are you a good observer?

Try this test.

Look at the picture for 30 seconds. Focus on the details. Then turn to page 52 and answer the questions.

Can you solve problems?

Problem 1: What are the next two numbers in this sequence?

1   2   4   7   11   ?   ?

Problem 2: The strange man on the top floor

Every day, a man who lives on the 20th floor of a block of flats gets the lift down. But when he comes home, he always gets out at the 13th floor and walks up the rest. Why?

Problem 3: What's that word?

This is a famous clue from a crossword:

Clue: A B C D E F G .... P Q R S T U V W X Y Z

Can you work out the answer?

It's a common 5-letter word with the middle letter "t": __ __ t __ __

 **Eddie Chapman**

In the Second World War, the Germans wanted to invade Britain. They needed to find out secret information, such as where important factories were. The British wanted to stop the invasion and damage German plans to attack other countries.

Both sides needed spies to find out what was going on.

Eddie Chapman, nicknamed "Agent Zigzag", worked for Germany *and* Britain. He had skills both sides needed: he was a good liar, he knew about explosives, and he learned things quickly.

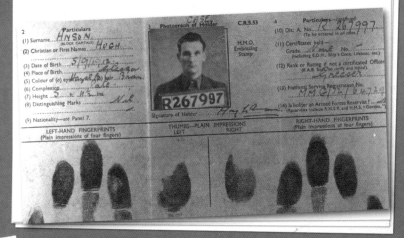

Eddie Chapman dressed in German uniform for this 1961 photo.

Inside info

Dates: 1914–1997

AKA: Edward Edwards, Arnold Thompson, Edward Simpson and Fritz!

Eddie's British boss named him Agent Zigzag because he kept going from one side (British) to the other (German) and back again!

How did Eddie become a spy?

Eddie was part of a well-known "jelly gang" in London in the 1930s. He was an expert at blowing up safes. (They were called jelly gangs because they used the explosive **gelignite**.)

He fled to the island of Jersey when he realised the police were after him.

There, he was caught and put in prison.

But then the Germans invaded Jersey!

Eddie offered to spy for them. It meant he could get out of jail. The Germans accepted. They even paid him money to do it.

Eddie was trained in explosives, radio communications and how to parachute out of a plane.

Eddie becomes a double agent

The Germans parachuted Eddie into England. His job was to blow up an aircraft factory. But he decided it was safer to work for the British, so he became a double agent, pretending to spy for the Germans while actually working for the British.

He went back to the Germans and told them he had destroyed the aircraft factory. It was a lie.

In fact, the British Secret Services set up fake scenes to make it look like the factory had been destroyed.

Here is a photo of one of them.

Eddie's next mission

Next, the Germans gave Eddie a bomb hidden in a piece of coal. His task was to plant it on a British ship off the coast of Portugal. But Eddie handed the bomb over to the captain.

For some reason, the Germans never noticed that the ship wasn't destroyed!

Eddie zigzags back to Britain

Finally, the Germans sent him back to Britain. Eddie's job was to send secret reports back to Germany, telling them how accurate German flying bombs were. But he sent back false reports lying about where the bombs had landed, so the next set of bombs missed their targets.

Near the end of the war, Eddie became bored and turned to crime again, so MI6 sacked him.

But his fame meant that a film called *Triple Cross* was made about his life.

Inside info

After the war, Eddie became good friends with the German spy boss whom he had tricked. He even went to Eddie's daughter's wedding!

RESTRICTED INFORMATION   RESTRICTED INFORMATION   RESTRICTED INFORMATION

Great gadgets

Spies have always had special gadgets to help them.

Have you seen Q in the James Bond films? His job is to give Bond gadgets that will trick his enemies.

Most famous of all? Bond's Aston Martin car.

Rear bullet-proof shield

Machine guns under headlamps

Ejector-seat

FMP 7B

Gadgets have always played a big part in real spying, too.

James Bond's gadget man, Q, got his name from the real-life Q Branch. This was a section of MI6. The head of it was even called Q!

One of Q Branch's inventions was a matchbox camera. Can you see the tiny hole for the lens in the side?

MI6 were not the only ones using matchbox cameras. The Germans had them too. Here is what the actual camera inside the matchbox looked like.

Look at this pencil with a sharp blade inside it.

The pencil has been hollowed out, so you can see the blade. Normally, it would have been hidden.

The blade had a piece of string wrapped around it. By pulling the string, you could get the blade out quickly.

Inside info

Used by: Special Operations Executive (SOE)

When: Second World War

 # The poison-tip umbrella

What is the best weapon for a spy to use? Perhaps an everyday object, such as a cup or a pencil – or even the tip of an umbrella?

This is how the man below was killed in 1978.

His name was Georgi Markov.

Markov was a Bulgarian writer. He had written plays and articles that criticised the communist Bulgarian government during the Cold War.

He was forced to leave Bulgaria and come to the UK.

But he continued to write. So, the Bulgarian spy services sent one of their agents to the UK, possibly with the help of the Russian KGB.

The agent brought this weapon – or something like it.

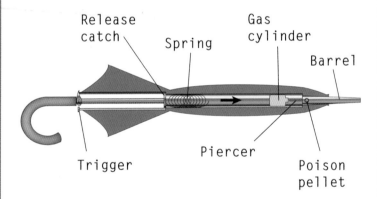

Release catch
Spring
Gas cylinder
Barrel
Piercer
Trigger
Poison pellet

As Markov waited for a bus on Waterloo Bridge in London, he felt a sharp sting in his thigh.

He turned round and saw a man picking up an umbrella from the ground.

Later that day, he noticed a red pimple.

The pain got worse.

He went to hospital, but died three days later.

When doctors examined his dead body, they found a small pellet in his leg.

This pellet had been filled with a poison called **ricin**.

This is a lethal poison from the castor-oil plant. Only a tiny amount, like a few grains of salt, is needed to kill someone.

Ideal for the tip of an umbrella …

Inside info

The main suspect has never been brought to justice!

RESTRICTED INFORMATION   RESTRICTED INFORMATION

Tricks and disguises

Spies have always used **disguises**, but how far would you go to change your appearance? Would you …

… cut off or dye your hair

… grow a beard (difficult for a girl!)

… wear a wig

… change your clothing

… have plastic surgery?

In the Second World War, the Special Operations Executive had workshops to produce false documents, clothing and disguises.

Here is the badge from a false German uniform they made.

Fake shoes

Leaving footprints is one way spies can get caught.

But what if you were able to leave *fake* footprints?

During the Second World War, the Special Operations Executive designed these "feet" to leave false tracks.

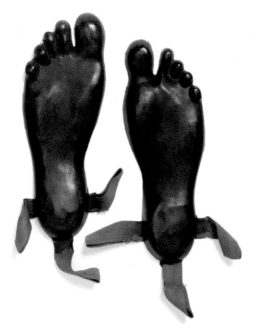

Spies wore them over their ordinary shoes during beach landings in the Far East. The idea was that the tracks would look like a local walking barefoot.

The man who never was

In 1943, the British intelligence services created the ultimate disguise: a man who had never existed.

The idea was to trick the Germans into thinking Britain would attack Greece and the Italian island of Sardinia. In fact, the British were planning to attack Sicily.

How did they do it?

First, the British got a dead body and gave him a name, Major Bill Martin. They dressed Bill in military clothes with "secret" letters about the invasion inside the pockets.

They kept the body fresh in a special container with dry ice. Then they launched it into the sea from a submarine off the coast of Spain.

What happened next?

The Spanish found the body and passed it on to the Germans.

The Germans were convinced Major Martin was real because he had photos of a girlfriend, Pam, bills from real shops, tickets, an ID card and even a letter from his girlfriend and father!

Did it work?

Yes! Hitler sent some of his forces to Sardinia instead of Sicily. When Britain and her allies attacked Sicily in July 1943, the Germans weren't there in large numbers to defend it.

Inside info

The mission was called "Operation Mincemeat".

RESTRICTED INFORMATION   RESTRICTED INFORMATION   RESTRICTED INFORMATION

Getting caught

What happens to you if you are caught?

1 You might be "turned".

This means you swap sides and become a double agent. Mathilde Carré was a French Resistance fighter in the Second World War. She and others plotted against the Nazi occupation.

The Nazis caught Mathilde and she began to work for them. Eventually she was found out. After the war, she was sentenced to twenty years in jail by a French court.

2 You might decide to take poison pills.

Agents were often given poison pills in case they were caught. These had two purposes – to stop them being tortured, and to stop them giving secrets away.

This necklace contained a cyanide pill.

3 You might be put to death.

Ethel and Julius Rosenberg were Americans who spied on their own country in the 1940s. They were accused of passing on information about America's atomic bomb to the Russians.

The American government put them on trial and they were executed by electric chair in 1953.

4 You might be sent home.

Russian spy Anna Chapman was caught in the US in 2010 and confessed to being a spy. She was sent back to Russia, where she became a TV celebrity!

 **Carl Lody**

Who was he?

Lody was a German spy in the First World War. He had lived in America and had an American wife, so he spoke perfect English.

His first mission in Britain was to send back reports about British ships as they were leaving port. He sent a telegram in code and, soon after, a German U-boat sank a British ship called *HMS Pathfinder*.

Lody's false name was Charles A. Inglis. Imagine you were sent as a spy to Germany. What name would *you* choose?

A deadly mistake

Unfortunately, Lody wrote some of his letters in German, and didn't bother to use a code!

He then went to Ireland but was arrested. Police found German coins and letters in German in his hotel room.

Later, police also found his coat with his real name inside and the name of the shop in Berlin it came from!

Death

Lody was taken to London, tried and executed by an 8-man firing squad in the Tower of London on 6 November 1914.

Secret codes

Do you ever use your own secret codes or language with friends?

If you think about it, secret codes are all around us.

But how do spy organisations use them?

Of course, if you're a spy, you can't send secret information in the normal way. It might be captured or intercepted by your enemies.

You can't just write:

ARMY ATTACK ON CITY ON 7th JAN

But you *can* use a code which only you and the person you are sending it to know.

For example:

CTOA CVVCEM QP EKVA QP 9vj LCP

... is a bit more difficult to understand.

How does the code above work?

Codes used by spies

Substitution ciphers

This is where one letter is replaced by another letter or by a number.

You can make these codes with a **decoder ring**:

By moving the smaller circle round, you can create new ciphers each time.

Transposition ciphers

Here, the words might stay the same but you use a shape or path to "read" them. For example, you might put your message into a box shape.

If your fellow spy knows the order or shape (that it's a 5 by 4 box and needs to be read left to right) you could send them:

WOYA   ARTR   IMHK   TEEE   FBMT

As long as they know the system – that these sets of letters are columns from left to right – then the message can be deciphered.

W	A	I	T	F
O	R	M	E	B
Y	T	H	E	M
A	R	K	E	T

The Enigma Codes

In the Second World War, the Germans had very clever codes they used to contact their U-boats and planes.

Enigma means a mystery or puzzle.

How did the codes work?

The codes were produced on machines that look like old fashioned typewriters. Unfortunately, there were lots of Enigma machines, and the Germans updated them all the time.

This is one of the German Enigma machines.

Who tried to crack the codes?

Some Polish code breakers and a huge team of code breakers who worked at a place called Bletchley Park near Milton Keynes. The operation to crack the codes was called "Ultra".

Did they succeed?

Fortunately, the British captured some of the code books from German ships. They also listened in to secret conversations. This gave the code breakers the information they needed to crack the code.

Did cracking the codes help to win the war?

By 1945, British code breakers were able to understand nearly all German messages.

At the end of the war, British Prime Minister Winston Churchill called the code breakers "the geese that laid the golden eggs".

This is a famous poster from the Second World War. "Mum" means "quiet". What do you think the poster was warning people about?

Mata Hari

Throughout history, there have been many female spies.

Name: Known as Mata Hari, her real name was Margaretha Zelle.

Who did she spy for?: The Germans against the French, in the First World War.

Skills: She was a dancer and had lovers in the French military.

What did she find out?: She passed on the names of French spies to the Germans, although she always denied this.

What happened to her?: Her code name – H21 – was discovered and she was shot by a firing squad in 1917.

Odette Hallowes

Odette and Peter Churchill;
they married after the war.

Name: Odette Hallowes

Who did she spy for? The British against the Germans in France in the Second World War.

Skills: She was British but came from France. She was trained by the Special Operations Executive in codes and sabotage (destroying things!).

What did she find out?: She mainly worked as a messenger for another SOE agent, Peter Churchill, and brought him money to help the French Resistance.

What happened to her?: She and Peter were betrayed by a double agent in 1943. They were sent to Paris, where they were tortured by the Nazis. But she always kept the story going that she and Peter were married and that Peter was the nephew of Winston Churchill.

Odette was sent to a concentration camp, yet somehow she survived the war. She was given an award for her bravery.

Violette Szabo

In 1942, Violette Szabo, a young woman who was half-French, learnt that her husband had been killed by German forces.

Violette decided to help fight the Nazis, and joined the SOE, like Odette.

She was given training in codes, explosives, unarmed combat and sabotage.

Her first mission

She was parachuted into France on 5 April 1944. She met with the local Resistance fighters and worked with them to sabotage roads and bridges. She also sent back messages by wireless about the location of weapons factories.

What happened to her?

In June 1944, on her second mission, Violette was stopped at a roadblock and captured by the Germans.

After being interrogated and tortured, she was sent to a concentration camp and executed. She was only 23. After her death, she was also given an award for bravery.

Inside info

A popular film of Violette's life, *Carve Her Name with Pride*, was released in 1958. The film still above shows her being captured.

Spying today

What new gadgets do today's spies use?
And what will they use in the future?

Drones

A **drone** is an aircraft or ground vehicle without a
pilot or driver. It is controlled remotely and can be
used to watch and send back reports on the enemy.

Inside info

US scientists have developed an app that allows
users to control a drone from their phone!

Face-recognition technology

Want to stop people getting into your secret bunker?
Then forget about passwords. There are now doors
with locks that only allow
access if they recognise
your face, eyes or
palm prints.

> Identity matched
> access granted

 **The Moscow rock**

Devices hidden inside apparently natural objects have often been used by spies. But not always with success.

In 2006 the Russian security services found out that British spies were using a "rock" to hide electronic equipment. The gadget in the rock sent information to pocket computers held by British spies as they walked past!

The "rock"

The computer hidden inside

 Can you think of a new gadget or weapon to help spies today? Something that would not be detected …

Is spying the job for you?

You have read about the different things real spies have to do, and about the risks they take. Is it a job you could do?

Think about the danger (imagine being caught!), but also the thrills.

Think about the spying jobs where you spend most of your time in an office. Would you like that?

Think about the heroes and the villains.

Do you have what it takes?

Questions about page 16

1 What wild animal can be seen in the top right of the picture?

2 What colour top is the third figure from the left wearing? She is the one walking into the shop.

3 What is the name of the shop with the orange sign?

4 What does it say on the Union Jack sign at the top of the images?

A) World Famous Market

B) World Famous Meerkat

C) World's Cheapest Market

5 How many tailor's dummies can be seen in the shop window?

Problem 1

The next two numbers are 16 and 22 (the gap between each number is +1 each time: 1 to 2 [gap is 1] 2 to 4 [2] 4 to 7 [3], etc.).

Problem 2

The man gets out on the 13th floor of the block because he is very short in height and can't reach the button for the 20th floor.

Problem 3

The answer is WATER. The clue doesn't show the letters from "H to O" – H_2O is the chemical symbol for water!

Reader challenge

Word hunt

1 On page 4, find an adjective that means "made up" or "imaginary".

2 On page 21, find an adjective that means "false".

3 On page 37, find a verb that means "put to death".

Text sense

4 Why can't you send secret information in the normal way if you are a spy? (page 39)

5 Give one example of a code used by spies and explain how it works. (pages 40–41)

6 How were British code breakers able to crack the codes used by the Germans? (page 43)

7 Why do you think spies like Odette and Violette were tortured? (pages 46–49)

8 What would be the advantage of using a drone? (page 50)

Your views

9 Did you find the book interesting?
Give reasons.

10 Think of two advantages and two
disadvantages of working as a spy.
Give reasons.

Spell it

With a partner, look at these words and then cover
them up.

● spy
● enemy
● ally

Take it in turns for one of you to read the words
aloud. The other person has to try and spell each
word. Check your answers, then swap over.

Try it

Would you like to be a spy? Would you make a
good spy? Discuss this with a partner. Think about
your answers to Question 10 and read the first few
paragraphs on page 52 again to give you ideas.

William Collins's dream of knowledge for all began with the publication of his first book in 1819. A self-educated mill worker, he not only enriched millions of lives, but also founded a flourishing publishing house. Today, staying true to this spirit, Collins books are packed with inspiration, innovation and practical expertise. They place you at the centre of a world of possibility and give you exactly what you need to explore it.

Collins. Freedom to teach.

Published by Collins Education
An imprint of HarperCollins*Publishers*
77–85 Fulham Palace Road, Hammersmith, London W6 8JB

Browse the complete Collins Education catalogue at **www.collinseducation.com**

Text by Mike Gould
© HarperCollins*Publishers* Limited 2012

Series consultants: Alan Gibbons and
Natalie Packer

10 9 8 7 6 5 4 3 2 1
ISBN 978-0-00-748478-2

British Library Cataloguing in Publication Data.
A catalogue record for this publication is available from the British Library.

Commissioned by Catherine Martin
Edited and project-managed by Sue Chapple
Picture research and proofreading by Grace Glendinning
Design and typesetting by Jordan Publishing Design Limited
Cover design by Paul Manning
Text checked by Terry Charman

Published in association with Imperial War Museums

Acknowledgements

The publishers would like to thank the students and teachers of the following schools for their help in trialling the Read On series:

Southfields Academy, London
Queensbury School, Queensbury, Bradford
Langham C of E Primary School, Langham, Rutland
Ratton School, Eastbourne, East Sussex
Northfleet School for Girls, North Fleet, Kent
Westergate Community School, Chichester, West Sussex
Bottesford C of E Primary School, Bottesford, Nottinghamshire
Woodfield Academy, Redditch, Worcestershire
St Richard's Catholic College, Bexhill, East Sussex

The publishers gratefully acknowledge the permission granted to reproduce the copyright material in this book. While every effort has been made to trace and contact copyright holders, where this has not been possible the publishers will be pleased to make the necessary arrangements at the first opportunity.

The publisher would like to thank the following for permission to reproduce pictures in these pages (t = top, b = bottom, c = centre, l = left, r = right):

p 2 c.Paramount/Everett/Rex Features, p 4 c.MGM/Everett/Rex Features, p 5 c.Focus/Everett/Rex Features, p 6 Modesty Blaise is © 2011 Associated Newspapers/Solo Syndication. Reproduction by arrangement with Titan Books Ltd., p 7 c.MGM/Everett/Rex Features, p 8 INTERFOTO / Alamy, p 9 Hulton Archive/Getty Images, p 12 Jim Bowen/Flickr, p 13 Federal Bureau of Investigation, p 14 c.Paramount/Everett/Rex Features, p 15 photo courtesy of Trevor Pateman, p 16 Mike Kemp/In Pictures/Corbis, p 18 © www.heritage-images.com, p 19 Popperfoto/Getty Images, p 21 The National Archives, p 23 Moviestore Collection/Rex Features, p 24 Sipa Press/Rex Features, p 25br © 2012 by AUCTION TEAM BREKER, Cologne, Germany (www.Breker.com), p 25c Anthony Devlin/PA Wire, p 27 Rex Features, p 29 Keystone/Getty Images, p 33 The National Archives, p 34t Keystone/Hulton Archive/Getty Images, p 35t NY Daily News via Getty Images, p 35b ZUMA Wire Service/Alamy, p 36 INTERFOTO/Alamy, p 37 The National Archives, p 38cl Madlen/Shutterstock, p 45 WikiMedia Commons, p 46 Central Press/Getty Images, p 49 Pictorial Press Ltd/Alamy, p 50t Tech. Sgt. Erik Gudmundson/WikiMedia Commons, p 50b Tyler Olson/Shutterstock, p 51 Ren-TV/Pressphotos/Getty Images.

The following images have been provided courtesy of Imperial War Museums, London:

p 20: H_022943, p 22: CL 3433, p 26: WEA 004147, p 30: INS 43105, p 31: EQU 012207, p 34b: EPH 010078, p 40: COM_000476, p 42: MH_027178, p 44: IWM_PST_004095, p 48: HU_016541
p 47: Interactive motion comic frame provided courtesy of Imperial War Museums and ISO (isodesign.co.uk) and used with permission from the illustrator, John McCrea (www.johnmccrea.com).